ENORA
and the black crane

Arone Raymond Meeks

SCHOLASTIC
HARDCOVER

SCHOLASTIC INC.
NEW YORK

Library of Congress Cataloging-in-Publication Data

Meeks, Arone Raymond.
    Enora and the black crane / Arone Raymond Meeks.
      p.   cm.
    Summary: Enora follows a shimmering band of colors deep into the rain forest, where an act of violence against a crane changes him forever.
    ISBN 0-590-46375-6
    [1. Rain forests — Fiction. 2. Cranes (Birds) — Fiction. 3. Wildlife conservation — Fiction.] I. Title.
PZ7.M51288En   1993
[E] — dc20   92-32123
                                          CIP
                                          AC

12 11 10 9 8 7 6 5 4 3 2 1   3 4 5 6 7 8/9

Printed in the U.S.A.   37

First Scholastic printing, September 1993

Long ago when the world was new,
there lived a young man named Enora.

Enora and his people lived in a rain forest filled with wonderful food. Delicious fruit hung on the trees and the rivers were full of fish.